Together for KWANZAA

by Juwanda G. Ford ◆ illustrated by Shelly Hehenberger

For my grandmother Lillie Mae Ford, wishing we were always together.—J.G.F.

To Flora Leptak-Moreau, for your honesty and enthusiasm.—S.H.

Author's Note: This story tells how Kayla and her family celebrate Kwanzaa. Some families may have different Kwanzaa traditions, but all Kwanzaa celebrations are special in their own way!

A Random House PICTUREBACK® Book

Random House 🏠 New York

Text copyright © 2000 by Random House, Inc. Illustrations copyright © 2000 by Shelly Hehenberger. All rights reserved under International and Pan-American Copyright Conventions. Published in the United States by Random House, Inc., New York, and simultaneously in Canada by Random House of Canada Limited, Toronto.
www.randomhouse.com/kids
Library of Congress Cataloging-in-Publication Data
Ford, Juwanda G. Together for Kwanzaa / by Juwanda G. Ford ; illustrated by Shelly Hehenberger. p. cm.
SUMMARY: While celebrating Kwanzaa and its many traditions with her parents, Kayla hopes that her big brother Khari will get home from college before the holiday is over. ISBN 0-375-80329-7 (trade) — ISBN 0-375-90329-1 (lib. bdg.) [1. Kwanzaa—Fiction. 2. Brothers and sisters—Fiction. 3. Afro-Americans—Fiction.] I. Hehenberger, Shelly, ill. II. Title. PZ7.F7532115To 2000 [E]—dc21 99-46535
Printed in the United States of America July 2000 10 9 8 7 6 5 4 3 2 1
PICTUREBACK, RANDOM HOUSE and colophon, and PLEASE READ TO ME and colophon are registered trademarks of Random House, Inc.

It was the first day of Kwanzaa, and Kayla was sad. Her big brother, Khari, could not come home for the holidays because a heavy snowstorm had closed all the roads around his school. Kayla always missed Khari while he was away, but this was worse than ever.

Now they would have to start Kwanzaa without him.

Kwanzaa was Kayla's favorite time of year. She loved celebrating her African heritage and doing special things with her family. But how could she enjoy Kwanzaa this year if Khari was not part of it?

Kayla tried to cheer up. After dressing in colorful African clothing, she began to set the Kwanzaa table. First, she put down the *mkeka* (muh-KAY-kuh), a traditional straw mat. On top of the *mkeka*, she placed the *kinara* (kee-NAH-ruh), a Kwanzaa candle holder. The *kinara* holds seven candles, one for each night of Kwanzaa: a black candle in the middle, three red candles on the left, and three green candles on the right. The colors stand for different things: black for the African-American people, red for their struggles, and green for hope and a good future.

Each night of Kwanzaa, families light candles and celebrate one of the seven Kwanzaa principles, which are ideas that help people to be strong. The principles help to guide them through Kwanzaa but are practiced all year long. There is a different principle for each day of Kwanzaa.

Every year Kayla and Khari would share the Kwanzaa greeting.

"Habari gani?" (huh-BAH-ree GAH-nee) Khari would say. The greeting is from the Swahili language. It means "What is happening today?" Kayla would answer with the Kwanzaa principle for that day. Many Swahili words are used during Kwanzaa.

Kayla sighed. It just wouldn't be the same without Khari there tonight!

Kayla's parents helped her place fruits and vegetables on the *mkeka*. The fruits and vegetables are called *mazao* (muh-ZAH-o). They represent the harvest and the importance of working together.

"Here is the corn!" said Kayla.

"Do you remember the Swahili word?" her mother asked.

"Muhindi," (moo-HEEN-dee) Kayla answered. "The *muhindi* represents the children in the family." She put two ears of corn next to the other Kwanzaa symbols. One for her and one for Khari.

When the table was ready, Kayla's mother helped her
light the black candle. Kayla knew that they would light a
red candle the second night, a green one the next night, and
so on, until all the candles were burning on the last night.

Since Khari was not there, Kayla's father greeted her. *"Habari gani?"* he said.

Kayla answered with the first principle of Kwanzaa. *"Umoja!"* (oo-MOE-juh) she said. *Umoja* means unity.

Kayla's father poured a few drops of water from the *kikombe cha umoja* (kee-KOME-bay chah oo-MOE-juh), or unity cup, to remember and honor their ancestors. At Kwanzaa, everyone drinks from the unity cup to celebrate family and community unity.

Kayla and her family practiced unity all year by spending time together as a family. Kayla especially loved family movie night. They would rent movies and eat pizza and popcorn all night long. Thinking about movie night made Kayla miss Khari even more.

The next night, Kayla's father lit the black candle and the first red candle. He said, *"Kujichagulia,"* (koo-jee-chah-goo-LEE-yuh) which is the second principle of Kwanzaa. It means self-determination, or deciding what you want to be and do.

Kayla decided that she wanted
to go to college just like Khari,
and study to become a scientist.

On the third night, the phone rang just as Kayla was lighting the first green candle. It was Khari!

"Habari gani?" Khari said.

"Ujima!" (oo-JEE-muh) Kayla answered. *Ujima* is the third principle of Kwanzaa. It means working together and being responsible.

On the third night, the phone rang just as Kayla was lighting the first green candle. It was Khari!

"*Habari gani?*" Khari said.

"*Ujima!*" (oo-JEE-muh) Kayla answered. *Ujima* is the third principle of Kwanzaa. It means working together and being responsible.

Kayla decided that she wanted
to go to college just like Khari,
and study to become a scientist.

One way Kayla and her family practiced *ujima* during the year was by participating in her school's bake sale. The teachers, parents, and students all worked together to raise money for the community.

The black candle, one green candle, and two red candles were lit on the fourth night. Kayla was really happy tonight. The roads were cleared and Khari was on his way home. The principle for the fourth night of Kwanzaa is *ujamaa* (oo-JAH-muh). *Ujamaa* means cooperative economics, or supporting African-American businesses. Kayla and her parents loved shopping in Tubman Square, where African-Americans sold handmade jewelry, hats, and clothes.

The phone rang, and Kayla ran to answer it.

"Hi, Khari, are you almost home?" she asked.

Khari explained that his car had broken down on the way. It would take a few days to fix. Kayla burst into tears. There were only three days of Kwanzaa left. Khari would miss everything!

"Don't cry, sweetie," Khari said. "I'll see you real soon. I promise!"

On the fifth night, Kayla's mother lit the candles. Today's principle was *nia* (NEE-yuh), or purpose.

Kayla decided that her purpose was to be the best little sister she could be. She made Khari a special Kwanzaa scrapbook, telling him all about how the family celebrated this year.

Kuumba (koo-OOM-bah), or creativity, is the principle for the sixth day of Kwanzaa. After the last red candle was lit, Kayla and her parents made lots of decorations for the *karamu* (kuh-RAH-moo) that night. The *karamu* is a feast where families celebrate with friends and loved ones.

Kayla made a flag using the Kwanzaa colors. It was black, red, and green, just like the candles in the *kinara*.

Soon there was a knock at the door. Kayla ran to answer it.

"Khari!" she yelled as she opened the door wide.

"No, not Khari. But Grandma and Grandpa are here!"

Kayla was glad to see her grandparents, but she couldn't help being disappointed that Khari still had not arrived. She kept hoping that somehow he'd get home before Kwanzaa was over.

There were many knocks on the door from friends and family. It was hard to be sad with so many people around!

Everyone was enjoying the *karamu*. There was so much food, they had to have a separate table just for desserts.

No one heard Khari at the front door, so he just walked right in. Kayla squealed with delight when she saw him.

"You made it!" Kayla said, smiling.

"I took a taxi to a bus," he answered. "Just to see you!"

Kayla hugged Khari as tight as she could.

"Imani," (ee-MAH-nee) Khari whispered on the last night of Kwanzaa. Tonight all the candles glowed brightly. *Imani* means faith, believing in yourself and others.

"I believe in our family," Kayla said as they opened their *zawadi* (zuh-WAH-dee), or gifts.

Kayla knew that *zawadi* should be handmade or educational. She gave everyone a photo of the family in a frame she had made from old newspapers.

Everyone loved their *zawadi*—especially Khari!

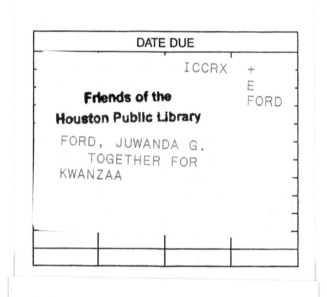